D0600761

First published in Belgium and Holland by Clavis Uitgeverij, Hasselt – Amsterdam, 2015
Copyright © 2015, Clavis Uitgeverij

English translation from the Dutch by Clavis Publishing Inc. New York
Copyright © 2016 for the English language edition: Clavis Publishing Inc. New York

Visit us on the web at www.clavisbooks.com

Ducky and the Monsters written and illustrated by Lotje® (Lizelot Versteeg)
Original title: *Eendje en de monsters*
Translated from the Dutch by Clavis Publishing

ISBN 978-1-60537-285-3

This book was printed in January 2016 at Wai Man Book Binding (China) Ltd. Flat A, 9/F., Phase I,
Kwun Tong Industrial Centre, 472-484 Kwun Tong Road, Kwun Tong, Kowloon, H.K.

First Edition
10 9 8 7 6 5 4 3 2 1

Ducky and the
MONSTERS

Clavis

NEW YORK

This is Ducky.
Ducky is on his way home.
He walks cheerfully towards the forest.

But hey, this isn't just a normal forest!
This is the big **MONSTER FOREST**!

Do you think Ducky is afraid of monsters?

"Hi, Ducky!" says one black monster.
He has such **BIG EYES**!

But Ducky is not afraid.
He winks at the monster.

.lo, hello!" call **two green** monsters.

y have big **POINTY EARS**.

But Ducky is not afraid.
He whistles a nice song for the monsters.

"Achoo!" sneeze **three red** monsters.
They have such **WET NOSES!**

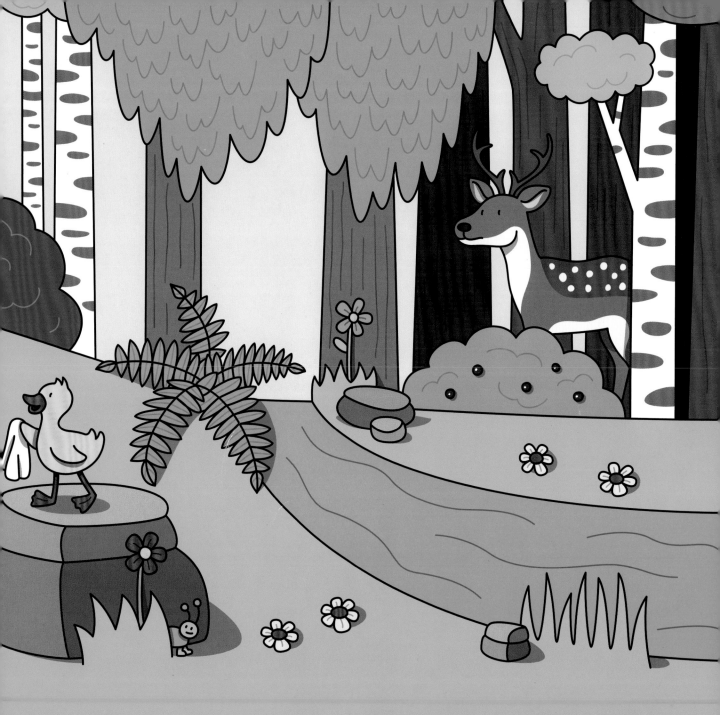

But Ducky is not afraid.
He quickly gives the monsters a tissue.

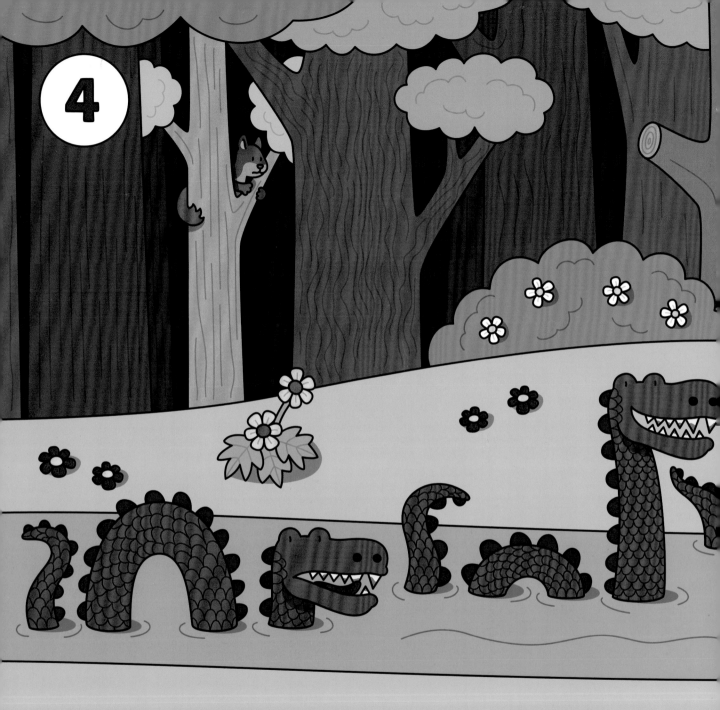

Four purple monsters swim in the water.
They have mouths filled with **SHARP TEETH**.

But Ducky is not afraid.
He helps the monsters brush their teeth.

"Look!" scream **five yellow** monsters.
They point with their **FAT FINGERS**.

But Ducky is not afraid. He gets the ball out of the water for the monsters.

Further down Ducky sees **six orange** monsters.
They have **MESSY HAIR!**

But Ducky is not afraid.
He styles the monsters' hair with a comb.

"Ducky! Ducky!" sing **seven white** monsters.
They wave their **THIN ARMS**.

But Ducky is not afraid.
He happily dances around with the monsters.

Eight brown monsters are hungry.
Their **BELLIES** growl loudly.

But Ducky is not afraid.
He picks some juicy apples for the monsters.

"Heeheehee!" Nine pink monsters giggle aloud.
They wiggle their **SMALL TOES.**

But Ducky is not afraid.
He tickles the soles of the monsters' feet.

Ten blue monsters skip around.
They have such **LONG LEGS**!

But Ducky is not afraid.
He cheerfully waddles between the monsters.

Finally Ducky is **HOME**!
He gladly jumps into the big pond.

The monsters wave one last time. "Bye, Ducky! Will you come and play again tomorrow?"